SHARE A STORY

The True Story of
Humpty Dumpty

Introduction

One of the best ways you can help
your children learn and learn to read
is to share books with them. Here's why:

• They get to know the **sounds**, **rhythms** and **words**
used in the way we write. This is different from how we
talk, so hearing stories helps children learn how to read.

• They think about the **feelings** of the characters
in the book. This helps them as they go about
their own lives with other people.

• They think about the **ideas** in the book. This helps
them to understand the world.

• Sharing books and listening to what your children
say about them shows your children that you care
about them, you care about what they think
and who they are.

Michael Rosen

Michael Rosen
Writer and Poet
Children's Laureate (2007-9)

First published 1987 by Walker Books Ltd
87 Vauxhall Walk, London SE11 5HJ

This edition published 2011

2 4 6 8 10 9 7 5 3 1

Text © 1987 Sarah Hayes
Illustrations © 1987 Charlotte Voake
Concluding notes © CLPE 2011

The right of Sarah Hayes and Charlotte Voake to be identified as author
and illustrator respectively of this work has been asserted by them in
accordance with the Copyright, Designs and Patents Act 1988

This book has been typeset in Goudy Educational

Printed in China

British Library Cataloguing in Publication Data:
a catalogue record for this book is available from the British Library

ISBN 978-1-4063-3509-5

www.walker.co.uk

The True Story of
Humpty Dumpty

Written by
Sarah Hayes

Illustrated by
Charlotte Voake

WALKER BOOKS
AND SUBSIDIARIES
LONDON · BOSTON · SYDNEY · AUCKLAND

Humpty Dumpty sat on a wall.
A horse came up to watch.
"Can you sit on this wall, horse?"
Humpty Dumpty said.

"Of course," said the horse.
And he did.

Then he wobbled and wobbled,
and then he fell off.

Humpty Dumpty laughed.
"Tee-hee," he said,
"you've hurt your knee."

Humpty Dumpty sat on the wall.
Another horse came up to watch.
"Can you stand on this wall, horse?"
Humpty Dumpty said.

"Of course," said the horse.
And he did.

Then he wobbled and wobbled,
and then he fell off.

Humpty Dumpty laughed.
"Oh dear," he said,
"you've hurt your ear."

Humpty Dumpty sat on the wall.
A man came up to watch.
"Can you stand on one leg
on this wall, man?"
Humpty Dumpty said.

"Yes," said the man, "I can."
And he did.

Then he wobbled and wobbled,
and then he fell off.

Humpty Dumpty laughed.
"Ho-ho," he said,
"you've hurt your toe."

Humpty Dumpty sat on the wall.
Another man came up to watch.
"Can you stand on one leg
and juggle with bricks
on this wall, man?"
Humpty Dumpty said.

"Well," said the man,
"I think I can."
  And he did.

Then he wobbled and wobbled,
and then he fell off.

Humpty Dumpty laughed.
"Go to bed," he said,
"you've hurt your head."

Humpty Dumpty sat on the wall.
The King came up to watch.
He saw his horses
and he saw his men.

And the King was terribly,
terribly cross.

"Come down," the King said.
"Come down from that wall."
But Humpty Dumpty said nothing at all.
He stood on one leg and juggled with bricks.
He did cartwheels and headstands
and all sorts of tricks.

Then he wobbled and wobbled,
and then he fell off.
CRASH!

And all the King's horses,

and all the King's men ...

put Humpty Dumpty together again.
And Humpty said, "After such a great fall
I'll never ever climb back on that wall."

But he did!

Sharing Stories

Sharing stories together is a pleasurable way
to help children learn to read and enjoy books.
Reading stories aloud and encouraging
children to talk about the pictures and join in
with parts of the story they know well are
good ways to build their interest in books.
They will want to share their favourite books
again and again. This is an important part
of becoming a successful reader.

The True Story of Humpty Dumpty is a playful picture-book version of a favourite nursery rhyme. Children who know the rhyme well will recognize the jokes and make connections with the original. Here are some ways you can share this book:

- The repeated words and phrases in the story encourage children to join in the reading. Make it a rhyming game by leaving space for them to guess and say the rhyming word or phrase.

- With books they know well, children can have a go at reading them to you. With time and practice they will get closer to matching the words written on the page. You can help build their confidence as readers by praising their early attempts rather than jumping in to correct them.

- Talking about books is part of being a reader. Children can ask questions and share their opinions about this version of the rhyme. They can talk about and sing other rhymes they know.

- Children will enjoy acting out the rhyme and it will be even more fun if you join in. They can use toys to act it out too.

SHARE A STORY
A First Reading Programme
From Pre-school to School

Beginnings – 2 years+

Early Steps – 3 years+

Next Steps – 4 years+

Taking Off – 5 years+

Sharing the best books makes the best readers

WALKER BOOKS

www.walker.co.uk